For Evan and George with love – M. R.

With love to Barbara and David – N. E.

PUFFIN BOOKS
UK | USA | Canada | Ireland | Australia | India | New Zealand | South Africa
Puffin Books is part of the Penguin Random House group of companies
whose addresses can be found at global.penguinrandomhouse.com.

puffinbooks.com

First published 2013
This edition published 2015
001

Goodnight Tractor

Michelle Robinson

Illustrated by **Nick East**

PUFFIN

The stars are out.
It's time for bed.
So say 'goodnight',
my sleepyhead.

Goodnight farmer.

Goodnight plough.

Goodnight trailer.

Goodnight cow.

Goodnight dog,

and goodnight sheep . . .

Goodnight tractor, time to sleep.

Goodnight combine.

Goodnight truck.

Goodnight
donkey.